# The Hunter Becomes The Hunted

Mohammed Umar

Illustrated by
Soukaina Lalla Greene

Salaam Publishing
London

First published in Great Britain 2016

Salaam Publishing

London

www.salaampublishing.com

Salaampublishing@gmail.com

# CONTENTS


*Chapter One:* **The Hunter's Dream**    1

*Chapter Two:* **The Hunter's Gift**    7

*Chapter Three:* **The Hunter's Trap**    14

*Chapter Four:* **The Hunter's Mistake**    26

*Chapter Five:* **Gorilla Tactics**    34

*Chapter Six:* **The Hunter Trapped**    42

*Chapter Seven:* **The Hunter Retreats**    54

*Chapter Eight:* **The Hunter Becomes the Hunted**    60

*And Finally …*    64

**For Salim, Karim and Nafisa**

I would like to thank the many people
who took an interest in and helped me with
this project. Fiza Aziz, Samira Mohamed Ali,
Yasmin Nouioua, Gabriel and Noah Basden,
Sue Nyanmjoh, Theo Mandic-Tyler,
Sulaiman Ibrahim, Jamila Heinecke,
Anne Rodford, Frank Bailey, Ama Biney,
Farouk Sohawon, Samad, Fajr and Safia Irfan.

I hope any omissions will be forgiven.

# CHAPTER ONE

# THE HUNTER'S DREAM

It was dawn. The early morning birds were twittering when the hunter woke up from his sleep. He rubbed his eyes and smiled. The hunter was happy. He had just had a delightful dream. In it he dreamt he went to a part of the neighbouring forest called *shakara* and successfully hunted four animals. It was a feat no man had achieved. He not only succeeded in hunting but dreamt that he also became the king of *shakara* and ruled over the animals.

Still lying in bed, the hunter could hear the voice of his father who had once said to him: "Whatever you do my son, don't go to *shakara* to hunt. You'd be lucky to leave the place alive.

The animals there are very intelligent." But the hunter blocked out his father's voice.

The voice he wanted to hear was the one that spoke to him in the dream. The voice whispered. "If you want to succeed in the forbidden forest, you must do what your ancestors didn't do. You need another way of thinking to succeed in the forest; you need more than one face. You should go there not as a hunter but as a normal human being who is just observing the forest and the animals. Go there not as someone who is going to threaten their existence but someone who will sustain the forest. Present yourself as a man of peace. Then use everything at your disposal including sweet language and a good image to win over their trust, especially the two leaders: the bearded monkey and the bald gorilla."

Still lying in bed he could still see in his mind the part of the dream where the animals carried him on their shoulders and were singing: *Long Live the King! Long Live the conqueror!*

He strongly believed the voice in his dream. It addressed him by his nickname, *the conqueror.*

"Go forth and conquer. *Shakara* is yours and everything in it," he heard the voice again before leaving his bed.

The hunter started
making preparations
in earnest. He made
sure his bows and
arrows were in perfect
shape. And that they
were disguised as
ordinary utensils. He
checked to make sure
his catapult was also in
good condition. The
conqueror – as he was

called by his peers, smiled as he wore a mask.
There was a grin on his face as he packed the
animal trap. "The animals in *shakara* are in for a
real surprise."

The hunter smiled at his reflection in the mirror.
"You are destined to be the conqueror of the
forest. This is the best present the animals will
ever receive. When they see themselves in the
mirror, they will be so delighted that they will not
pay attention to whatever I do," he muttered to
himself as he wrapped the mirror.

The hunter called his dog with a familiar whistle.
The dog responded with a short bark and wagged
its tail. "We're going to hunt in *shakara*." Upon
hearing this, the dog became restless and barked

loudly. "Don't worry," he assured the dog, "I had a pleasant dream and in it I received a well-developed plan. I strongly believe I'll succeed where no man has ever succeeded before."

The hunter and the dog arrived at the edge of *shakara* before sunset. They stood by the stream that was the boundary where he loudly laid out his plan. "First I will make sure I win the trust of the animals. Then I will hunt. My target is to hunt and kill four animals. This will create an atmosphere of fear. Once they are frightened, I can impose my will over them. One day I'll be the king of *shakara*. All the animals will bow to me and I will dominate and rule them."

The hunter and his dog waited patiently near a cave. When most of the bats had flown out that evening, the hunter sneaked into the cave and quickly and efficiently closed the only entrance. There were a few bats in the cave that flapped their wings helplessly as they tried to fly out.

The hunter settled down quickly. He concealed his bows and arrows and made sure the mask was nowhere to be seen. "Not even a bat can see any of my weapons." He brought out a cone-shaped hat he had made and wore it.

"You look different," the dog remarked.

"This is the way I want the animals to see and know me in *shakara*," he replied tying the strap under his chin. He sent the dog to look for and convey a message to the two leaders of the forbidden forest. "Tell the bearded monkey and the bald gorilla that I would like to talk to them."

The hunter then made a sign which he put up in front of the cave:

**I'M A FRIEND NOT A FOE<br>
HAVE NO FEAR!<br>
I'M ONE OF YOU<br>
ALL ANIMALS WELCOME**

I'M A FRIEND NOT A FOE
HAVE NO FEAR!
I'M ONE OF YOU
ALL ANIMALS WELCOME

# CHAPTER TWO

# THE HUNTER'S GIFT

The two leaders of *shakara* were waiting for the hunter under a tree. When he was ready, he wore his cone-shaped hat and walked out of the cave with a big smile on his face. He was also carrying the wrapped mirror. He adjusted his cone-shaped hat several times as he walked towards where the bearded monkey and the bald gorilla were waiting.

The bearded monkey fingered his beard and cast a suspicious look.

"I've come here as an observer and not to hunt. I'm here to help and not to harm. I'm a friend

not a foe. I've only one face – the human face.
I can heal the sick. I have the knowledge. I can
protect the animals. I have weapons but they
are for self defence. I'll be here for you day and
night. I bring with me only good things. No
forest is complete without the human being." He
paused. "I'm here to make this place the perfect
forest; a place where humans and animals live
in perfect harmony. You can identify me always
by my hat. I wear it all the time even when I'm
sleeping. It's called the hat of life."

The two leaders of *shakara* looked at each other
and nodded.

"I say it loud and clear. I'm one of you.
Remember this face; the human face. Trust
me. Believe me. I promise that I will do to you
only what I will do to myself. You are all safe
and please take this message of friendship and
assurance to all the animals in the forest."

The hunter adjusted his hat and unwrapped the
present. "I've brought this present for you. I
hope it amuses you as much as it amused me."
He gave them the mirror.

The bearded monkey and the bald gorilla
thanked him.

The monkey fingered his beard. "You're welcome
to stay in the cave and make your observation.
We hope you will leave us in peace and that
we all live in harmony. You may not know this
but we animals strongly believe in fairness. The
forest is big enough and our motto here is: *If
there's room for us, there's room for you.*"

"We humans call it mutual respect and peaceful
co-existence."

"We expect you to respect us," the gorilla added
smiling.

"Of course," the hunter assured them. "I
promise to mind my own business. Please feel
free to visit me. My door is always open."

The gorilla added smiling.
"We believe what you've just
said - that you are one of us.
We look forward to living
peacefully with a human in
our midst."

"Enjoy the mirror," the
hunter said and stepped back.

The two animals looked at
the mirror with their curious
eyes. When the gorilla saw

his reflection, he was aggressive, as though he had met a new primate. He soon calmed down and looked at himself closely. The gorilla oohed and aahed over his reflection. "So this is what my bald head looks like?" The monkey played with his reflection and even touched it and joked. "My beard looks really cool."

The hunter left the amused leaders of *shakara* as they admired themselves.

In the cave, the hunter removed his hat and burst out laughing. "These animals are so stupid," he said to himself. "I cannot believe how dumb these animals are. And these ones call themselves the leaders of the forest? Such stupid leaders will only make my life here very easy."

*"Rap tah tap, rap tah tap*
*The hunter is here to hunt*
*Rap tah tap, rap tah tap*
*Shakara will be mine forever!*
The hunter sang and danced in the centre of the cave. He was relieved and excited. He turned to his dog. "The next task is yours. Go out and befriend the animals. Pretend to be one of them and in the process get me as much information as possible. Understood?"

"Yes."

"I would like to know where they sleep."

"That's easy!"

"I'm interested in the antelopes and the deer."

"We'll sort them out, boss."

The hunter looked around the cave. "I'll start digging the secret tunnel from here soon."

"Wouldn't the animals suspect if you start digging?"

"No," he said with strong conviction in his voice. "First the mirror will distract them and secondly, they are too stupid to understand what I'll be doing," he said loudly.

"Why dig a tunnel?"

"You'll know when we use it."

The days and weeks passed without any incident. The dog would go out from time to time to explore the forest. When he was not secretly digging the tunnel, the hunter would also make sure he had his cone-shaped hat on and walked around the forest. Within a short period of time, he established a route and a routine for his daily walk.

"Thank you for the present," the gorilla said one afternoon.

"I thought you'd like it."

"Now I can see how bald my head is," he said rubbing his bald head.

"I'm not interested in the mirror," the monkey said.

******

"I never thought it would be so easy," the hunter confessed to the dog one morning. "The animals showed no opposition to us settling down in the cave. They have not noticed that I have dug a secret tunnel. The mirror was really a good way of diverting their attention. Soon, very soon, I will hunt and frighten them. Then I'll take control of *shakara*. In the near future, the monkey and the gorilla will invite me to be the leader. They'll put a crown on my head. *Long Live the King! Long Live the Conqueror. You shall rule over us forever.*"

He closed his eyes and could see himself being carried around *shakara* with a crown on his head – just as he had seen in his dream! This time the animals even bowed in reverence. *It's just a matter of time before my dream comes true.*

******

# CHAPTER THREE

# THE HUNTER'S TRAP

One day when the hunter went out for his usual walk, the bearded monkey and the bald gorilla looked at him from a safe distance.

"The human with the silly hat is coming," the gorilla said.

"I'm suspicious of him, you know," monkey replied in low voice. "I think he's up to something. My animal instincts tell me that he is not one of us."

"Yo Monkey! I was just about to tell you about my doubts. I think this human will hunt. I can feel it too. It's important we keep a safe distance and keep an eye on him."

******

Many days later, the hunter felt it was time to take the next step. It was time to set a trap. The conqueror brought out the animal snare he had made and concealed it in his clothes. When he was sure no animal was watching, the hunter laid the trap near where the antelopes sleep. He and the dog quickly disappeared into the cave under partial darkness.

"I hope the trap catches an antelope," he prayed.

The hunter – still making sure he was wearing his cone-shaped hat waited patiently in the cave. Soon they heard screams from afar that drew closer and closer.

"HELP! HELP! HELP! We have an emergency," the gorilla cried out in front of the cave.

The hunter rushed out to meet him. "What happened? How can I help you?"

"Follow me," the gorilla said and led the hunter into the forest. "We need your help. Something has caught an antelope and we don't know how to release it."

The hunter ran with the gorilla to where the monkey was standing helplessly looking at the trapped antelope. The hunter who was still panting looked closely at the distressed animal, which had suffered cuts and bruises. It was waiting to be put out of its misery.

"This is strange," the hunter said. "I've never seen anything like this before in my life but I think I can remove it."

The hunter slowly removed the animal snare. The monkey was watching closely. When he finished, the gorilla thanked him. "We are very grateful. What would we do without you?"

"I told you before and will tell you again. I came here to help not to harm. I'm not a hunter. I am one of you. I hope you believe me now."

"Now I trust you," the gorilla said smiling, rubbing his bald head.

The monkey asked for the animal snare. The hunter reluctantly gave it to him.

The moment the hunter stepped into the cave, he
burst out laughing with excitement! "The animals
fell for it! The leaders of the forest are so stupid.
Who else will place a trap except me and yet they
believe I'm one of them! It's time to take the next
step; time to hunt. They'll never suspect me."

The hunter brought out his bow and some
arrows. "What's more, the moon is full, which
is the most ideal condition for hunting in this
forest. Not too dark and not too bright," he said
to himself as he put on the mask.

At predawn when the hunter was sure most
antelopes would be sleeping, he and the dog
squeezed themselves through the narrow
tunnel. They emerged at the back of the cave in
complete darkness. The hunter instructed the
dog, "Take me to where the antelopes gather and
sleep and by the way, after the hunt, we'll take a
different route back to the secret tunnel. I don't
want my footprints to lead to the cave. Do your
best to cover my footprints, okay?"

"Okay," the dog said and barked.

The hunter and the dog walked slowly and
nervously into the dark forest. They followed a
particular path.

"The antelopes are not that far from here," the dog whispered.

"You go and hide in the bushes. I can find my way from here. The only face the animals must see is the mask," the hunter said and walked away silently into the forest.

The dog obeyed and hid in the bushes.

With his mask firmly on his face and armed with his bow and arrows, the hunter tiptoed toward the sleeping antelopes. When he was close enough to them he made some strange loud noise. The

antelopes started running. They scattered helter-skelter. The hunter waited. He saw the injured antelope struggle to run in vain.

The hunter aimed and released an arrow at the small antelope. It was hit in the neck and collapsed. The hunter took the animal and wrapped it up making sure there was no blood dripping on the ground. The dog came out of its hideout and obediently followed the hunter back to the cave making sure that all his footprints were cleverly concealed.

The hunter and the dog took another path back to the cave. First they crossed the stream onto another part of *shakara* and then crossed back downstream. The path they took went straight to the mouth of the secret tunnel. They squeezed themselves into the cave one after the other with the antelope small enough to get through.

The hunter escaped just in time before the bearded monkey and the bald gorilla arrived at the scene. They were both horrified by the news of the attack.

"I'm worried that we have a predator in the forest and we are becoming preys."

The monkey did not reply immediately. He shook his head. "This is bizarre. The animal that attacked the antelope had a weird face; a face not seen before."

When dawn eventually broke, the gorilla looked closely at the area but there were no footprints and no blood on the ground. The gorilla and the monkey looked at each other puzzled. "This is worrying," the gorilla said rubbing his bald head.

The monkey agreed. "We're dealing with a beast we don't know. Any other animal would have left clues like paw prints or would have dragged the antelope away thereby leaving drops of blood on the ground."

"Let's see what the human has to say."

Later that day, the two leaders waited for the hunter.

The monkey politely asked. "Did you hear about the attack on antelopes? Do you know anything about it? Did you see anything suspicious?"

The hunter replied. "I don't know anything about the attack. I did not hear or see anything

unusual. Actually, I'm not a nocturnal person.
I was sleeping all night,' he said smoothly and
continued his walk with his dog.

For the next several weeks, there was anxiety and
fear among the animals.

Just before the moon was full, the hunter told the
dog that they'd be hunting. "This time around
we'll go for a small deer."

At predawn when he was sure the deer would be
asleep, the hunter and the dog went out through
the narrow secret tunnel. They went straight to
where the deer were and the hunter frightened
them with his mask. There was pandemonium.
He killed, wrapped and brought back a small
deer. The dog ensured there were no footprints
and no drops of blood. Just as they did the first
time, they took another route back to the cave.
The deer was small enough to pass through the
secret tunnel.

The hunter could not believe his luck again. "I
didn't realise it would be so easy. My masterplan
is working well. Now it's time to think about
how to make the animals my subjects. To do
this, I have to do something magical, something
that will create fear, suspense and disbelief.
I have to do something that will frighten the

animals. I want them to look up to me for help and protection. Then, I'll use the opportunity to make them my subjects."

He clapped his hands in delight and danced in the cave.

*"Rap tah tap, rap tah tap*
*The hunter is here to hunt*
*Rap tah tap, rap tah tap*
*Shakara will be mine forever!*

The conqueror boasted. "I always knew I would succeed here. I can see those two animals who call themselves the leaders of *shakara* one day putting a crown on my head! They will shout *Long live the king! Long live the conqueror! You will forever rule over us!*

In the deep forest of *shakara*, the monkey and the gorilla sat looking at each other. "I've never felt like this," the monkey said as darkness fell. "Sometimes you feel something is coming; you feel danger whenever the sun sets."

"I know what you mean," the gorilla said with a sigh. "I also see a weird face here, a weird face there, where did this weird face come from? I feel as if I can see this weird face everywhere I look, yet I look and see nothing. When I close my eyes, I see so many weird faces, but when

I open them I see nothing." He paused. "Yo monkey why have we been attacked only since the human came?"

"That's right."

"I feel we should confront him."

"But we have no proof," the monkey said thoughtfully. "You see, the face the antelopes and deer saw was not human. Let's be patient. If he's the one, we'll catch him."

"How?" the gorilla asked.

"He's human. He'll make one mistake and we'll seize upon it."

"I agree but not convinced."

Days later the leaders of *shakara* were keeping vigil when the hunter appeared. The gorilla was impatient. He jumped down from the low branch of the tree and confronted him.

The hunter made a blank denial. He repeated smoothly. "I'm not a nocturnal person. Did you see a human face? I always wear my hat even in my sleep. Did they see this hat? I've no reason whatsoever to attack any animal. Believe me, I have only one face; the human face. I gave you a mirror to give you pleasure. I did not come here to cause any pain. I came here with only one motive and that is to sustain the forest."

"But why did the attacks happen only since you came here?" the gorilla asked.

"Coincidence."

The gorilla was silent. The hunter walked away.

The monkey and the gorilla continued to keep vigil over the forest. The night was unusually quiet. The bearded monkey broke the long silence. "If only we knew what or who is attacking us then we can use the knowledge passed on to us for generations to turn ourselves from preys into predators." He paused. "Knowing the enemy is important."

"Yes, it's very frustrating…"

The monkey continued. "Our ancestors fought off predators in many battles because first they knew them. Our problem now is that we don't even know who the predator is."

The gorilla sighed in agreement. "Predator with a face never seen before."

A branch fell nearby. The two leaders looked around nervously.

"First the antelope was attacked, then a deer. You feel a hand stretching to catch you at any moment. Or that something will hit you, especially at night. We cannot continue to live like this. Yo monkey! What shall we do?"

"Wait and hope."

# CHAPTER FOUR

# THE HUNTER'S MISTAKE

*Rap tah tap, rap tah tap*
*The hunter is here to hunt*
*Rap tah tap, rap tah tap*
*Shakara will be mine forever!*

The hunter sang his usual song one evening.

"Why are you so excited?" the dog asked.

"My dream is about to come true," he responded.

"How do you know?"

"I can feel it in my bones," the excited hunter said and brought out his mask, bow and arrow and catapult. He inspected his weapons as he usually did before going for a hunt. "The moon is full today and we're going to hunt."

"What are we going for this time?

"A deer! Yummy deer! I did it once, I can do it again and again," he boasted.

At predawn, the two walked out of the cave through the secret tunnel and headed deep into *shakara* under the cover of darkness and tall trees. The dog stopped long before they reached where the herd of deer was sleeping. The hunter tiptoed into the place and made a cracking noise. The deer woke up and ran in different directions.

The hunter did not wait to aim at a particular target. He released his arrow. It hit a big deer in the neck. The deer struggled. After a while it slowed down and fell to the ground.

The hunter was excited. "That was easy," he said as he prepared to take his catch back to the cave. He only realised he had a problem when he tried lifting the deer. "Oops, this is heavy."

Time was not on his side. He tried taking it away before the two leaders arrived at the scene. It was getting lighter by the minute. The hunter decided to drag the dead deer to the cave.

The conqueror did not take the long route back to the cave. He wanted to get inside as soon as possible. "Damn it," he muttered to himself. "We have a problem. This deer cannot pass through the tunnel."

As they always did since the attack on the animals had begun, the bearded monkey and the bald gorilla visited the scene immediately. When the day eventually broke, the sharp-eyed monkey soon spotted something. "Hang on," he said and gestured to the gorilla. "Look, there are footprints and drops of blood."

"Aha! That's interesting."

"The first time such clues have been left."

"Human footprints," the gorilla said several times looking at them.

The two leaders looked at each other in disbelief.
They closely examined the footprints and
followed them and the odd drop of blood. They
were shocked when the clues led them to the
cave. They stood there startled.

"Fresh human foot prints," the gorilla was
beginning to be angry. "We've been lied to.
We've been deceived by this human being.
This is betrayal."

"But hold on," the monkey cautioned. "Let's
not jump to a hasty conclusion. We're not
one hundred percent sure yet. It could be a
coincidence. Maybe another human being was
responsible and wanted to implicate him …"

"But there's only one human in *shakara*," the
gorilla interrupted.

"Let us give him the benefit of doubt until we have conclusive evidence that he is responsible for the attacks."

"What evidence do you need?"

"As far as we know he has only one face and the face the deer saw was not human."

"I don't care about further proof," the gorilla said fuming with anger.

He was stamping his feet heavily on the ground.

"What's the hullabaloo about?" the hunter asked outside the cave.

The gorilla angrily confronted him. "We've every reason to believe you are a predator hunting animals in the forest."

He responded calmly. "Listen guys, when the antelope was caught in a trap, I released it. So judge me by what I have done not what you think I might have done. As I have said many times, I have only one face; the human face. Was the herd of deer attacked by a human being?"

"No. But look there are fresh footprints that led us to this place."

"They could have been there for days. I walk round here every day."

The gorilla cast suspicious look at him. "I'm not convinced you're not responsible."

"Go away and leave me alone. We agreed to leave each other alone."

The two animals turned and walked away.

"Mutual respect and peaceful co-existence, please!" the hunter shouted. He followed them and drew a line on the ground. "From now on, no animal must cross this line. Don't come close to the cave again. There's a boundary. This is my territory!"

"Yo monkey, listen to this human talking about his territory."

"Just ignore him."

"What?" the gorilla asked loudly. "Your territory! A boundary!"

"Yes, my territory, my boundary and my cave."

"Who gave you the right to carve out a territory, draw a boundary and own the cave?"

"I don't need anyone's permission. If you think I am responsible for the attacks on the animals then I feel threatened. I have to protect myself," he said looking straight into the eyes of the gorilla. "I can make my own rules now. Who do you think you are?"

"What is wrong with this human?" the gorilla charged forward.

"You animals must learn to respect my territorial integrity."

"I cannot believe what I'm hearing."

After a short uneasy standoff, the monkey pulled the gorilla away. "There's time for everything.

This is not the time to argue and fight. We will find out who is responsible soon."

Would they?

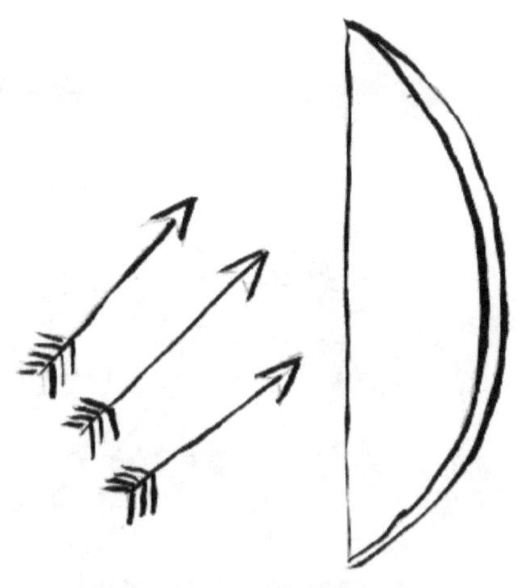

# CHAPTER FIVE

# GORILLA TACTICS

The two leaders of *shakara* retreated into the forest worried and angry.

"I know what to do," the gorilla said later nodding. "I'll wait for the human somewhere in the bushes tonight. If I suspect he's going to attack any animal I will attack him from behind."

The monkey thought for a while and then shook his head in disagreement. "No, don't."

"The best way to defend the animals is to attack the human first," the gorilla argued.

 "No! The gorilla tactic wouldn't work," the monkey shook his head doubtfully.

"Why?"

"He probably wouldn't come out tonight; so you'll be wasting your time. You will probably not be able to fight him alone and succeed; so you'll be wasting your energy. Haven't you noticed that the animals were attacked when there was a full moon?"

The gorilla nodded twice. "You're right."

The monkey continued. "A pattern is emerging. Let's be patient and watch out for more clues. Don't do anything just yet. Let us know the enemy well first. Let us understand what we're dealing with before engaging in any fight. Let's be patient …"

"I don't have the time to wait…" the gorilla interrupted angrily. "I've a duty to protect the forest and everything in it."

"Remember that he has some weapons."

"I've got thick skin. His weapon wouldn't harm me."

"Don't risk it," the monkey advised. "Let's wait and see."

"It's time to show him we are intelligent and can do things too." The gorilla went into the bushes and built body armour made of thick straw. "This should protect me from any sharp weapon the hunter might throw at me," he said showing off the body armour later. "I can take on this human being alone," he boasted and headed for the cave. The monkey followed.

The hunter was alerted by the barking dog. He rushed out with his bow and arrows. "Don't cross that line," he commanded in a loud voice. The gorilla ignored him. "What do you want?"

"I want to inspect the cave."

"No you can't."

"Why?"

"It's out of bounds to animals."

"What do you mean?"

"It's my private property."

"There's nothing like private property in *shakara*."

"I've declared it's my property and you can't inspect it."

"You must have something to hide then. I believe you are responsible for the attacks on the animals. Now allow me to inspect the cave." The gorilla said charging forward.

"STOP!" The hunter shouted. "Don't cross the line."

The gorilla ignored him.

The hunter aimed and shot at the gorilla as he crossed the line but the arrows hit the armour and fell on the ground. The gorilla was happy. "As you can see I'm well prepared for your weapons," the gorilla boasted and started to dance as he walked towards the hunter with confidence. The hunter brought out his catapult and put a rough stone in it and aimed at the advancing gorilla. The gorilla did not see it coming. The stone hit him near his right eye. He felt the pain instantly. He staggered and fell down.

The gorilla held his hand over his right eye which was bleeding profusely. "AAAARGH," the gorilla screamed. "The human has hurt me! The human has hurt me!"

The monkey rushed to the gorilla who groaned. "I cannot see! I cannot see!"

The hunter entered the cave and closed the door. "Sooner or later I have to show the animals that I mean business!" he said to the dog that was barking and shaking. "This is the right time to send the right message. I did not come here to play with the animals. I came here to conquer. This is the right time to introduce some human values and discipline. The animals must understand that the human armed with weapons can do whatever he wants and that the animals must suffer what they have to. The earlier they get that message the better. That's the rule and there's nothing they can do to change it." He paused. "I have taught the gorilla a lesson he will never forget. I can conquer and rule this place only if I instil fear in the animals. From now on, no animal dare cross the line and challenge me. They know that I have weapons and will use them. It does not matter anymore if they don't like me. What matters is that they fear me. Fear is good. Might is always right. *Long live the king. Long live the conqueror. Shakara will be mine forever.*"

******

Several days later, somewhere in the forest where the gorilla was recovering, the monkey took a deep breath and said. "We've lessons to learn. The human is most dangerous when confronted with the truth."

The gorilla nodded in agreement.

"You overestimated your strength."

"That's true."

"You underestimated his strength."

"That's equally true."

"Your gorilla tactic was wrong."

"You're right. Yo monkey, I did not expect him to be so cruel and vicious."

"He's a human being at the end of the day."

"If we cannot defeat the human in a face to face, tit-for-tat fight, what should we do?"

"I told you to be patient. Let's wait and watch. We animals did not survive this long by being angry and confrontational but by being patient and controlling our anger. There is a reason why humans have never succeeded in hunting and dominating animals here.  We've always been vigilant, resilient and used our ingenuity. These are the tools we use to change from preys to predators!"

"I understand what you mean."

"We need more time to understand him and his weapons. We didn't know he had a secret weapon for example. The weapon he used to inflict this injury on you. Somehow I'm sure we'll find a way to chase him out of the forest."

There was a long silence.

The monkey said moments later. "Let's change
tactics and trick the human."

"How?"

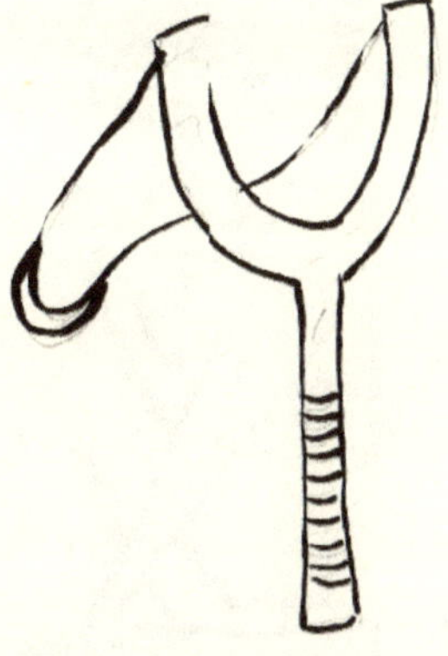

# THE HUNTER TRAPPED

"We the real leaders of the forest have decided to advise you to leave *shakara* and return to where you came from," the monkey told the hunter one afternoon. The hunter looked surprised. "This is not a place for you. Since you came, there have been mysterious attacks and some animals have disappeared in the middle of the night.  These incidents have led to so much fear and insecurity and now there is animosity between you and the gorilla."

The hunter ignored the monkey.

"It's you I'm talking to," implored the monkey.

"Why should I listen to you?" the hunter asked.

"I'm one of the leaders of *shakara*."

"You're just a monkey. I'm the king of *shakara*."

"What? King of where?"

"King of *shakara*," he repeated.

"What do you mean?"

"If you are the leaders, show me your symbols of authority."

"We shall soon show you. You are not the king."

"I'm the king and so can do what I want."

"Because you can doesn't mean you should."

"Nonsense," the hunter said, walking away.

"You should be careful in *shakara*."

"I don't need your advice. I don't care."

"Nothing lasts forever."

"Shut up."

"If you are powerful today, you may be weak tomorrow."

"Stop that empty monkey talk."

"Everything under the sun has it's time."

"What are you talking about?"

"Your time here will be over soon," predicted the monkey.

"Shut up!" He interrupted. "Go away and leave me alone."

"I just want to remind you that the hunter does become the hunted."

"Rubbish talk. I'm powerful and will remain so," he brandished his catapult.

"This is just a polite reminder."

"Go talk to the trees. I'm not going to listen to you."

"The hunter does become the hunted."

"Nonsense," the hunter dismissed the monkey.

As the monkey turned to leave, the hunter shouted. "Do me a favour."

"What's it?"

"Show me that you are the leaders of *shakara*. Show me your symbol of power. I have shown you mine."

"We shall come here in a couple of days to show you our symbol of power."

"I look forward to seeing them."

******

The monkey tapped the gorilla on the shoulder that evening. "The human wants us to show him our symbol of power; that we are the true leaders of the forest."

"Let's make beads and hang them on our bodies. That's easy."

"No, let's surprise him. Let us give him what he is not expecting."

"Like what?"

"Let us set a trap for him," the monkey said.

"Where do we get a trap?"

"I have one."

"Where did you get it?"

The monkey smiled. "Do you remember the trap that caught the antelope?"

The gorilla nodded.

"I have it and will adapt it to catch humans."

The gorilla was delighted. "Yo Monkey!" he exclaimed.

"I'll show him that this monkey means business," he added smiling.

The monkey took his time to adapt the trap.

They tried it a few times and were convinced it would work.

Just when they were finalising their plans, they received the news that a young antelope had been killed in an accident.

"That's exactly what we need," the monkey said excitedly. "A bait! And what's more it's full moon tonight. We might just be lucky and he'll come out to hunt tonight."

The monkey perfected the trap. The gorilla instructed some antelopes to walk from the cave to where they were setting the trap and made sure they urinated on the path.

After sunset – just before it became too dark, the monkey set the trap. The gorilla placed the corpse of the small antelope close to the trap.

"The human doesn't know what awaits him in *shakara*," the gorilla said with a smile.

"He's in for a real surprise."

The two leaders climbed a nearby tree and waited in silence.

Meanwhile, in the cave, the hunter was getting ready. He went through the usual routine and rituals and was pleased with his weapons. He could tell from the way it was barking that his dog was restless.

"The conqueror is ready! The conqueror always conquers. Don't worry. These animals are dumb. Since I came here, I have seen nothing to suggest that they have any intelligence at all. They have no capacity to think at all. I've shown the gorilla who is the boss. He has felt the effects of my power. From now on these stupid animals will shake when they see me. I've no fear at all. Let's go," he ordered. "I've hunted when the moon was full and succeeded. Not once. Not twice. I have confidence in my weapons too. I will succeed tonight. *Shakara* and every animal in it will be conquered."

The two went out through the front door of the cave.

The hunter wore his mask and followed the dog.

"I can smell urine of antelopes," the sniffing dog said.

"As always we're on the right path."

They continued their walk in the predawn darkness of the forest following the urine of the antelopes.

******

Meanwhile the two leaders of *shakara* waited nervously in a tree.

"I hope he comes out tonight," the gorilla whispered.

"My animal instincts tell me he'll be coming soon."

There was a period of silence.

"Yo monkey, you're right. I can see something approaching," the gorilla said with a trembling voice. "Can you see it?"

"Yes. Just remain calm. It's the human wearing a mask."

"This is unbelievable."

"Sssshhh! don't make any noise to distract him."

"Yo monkey! You're a genius," the gorilla whispered.

******

When the hunter and the dog reached a particular point, the dog stopped. "I can see a small antelope sleeping in the distance," the dog said and hid in the bushes as it always did when they went out hunting.

The hunter adjusted his mask. "That's good news. It's exactly what we need. Something small enough to wrap and take away! I'm lucky indeed," he smiled behind his mask. "Who said a man cannot hunt four animals in *shakara*? This is my fourth."

The hunter meanwhile took careful steps tiptoeing towards the bait. He was so mesmerised by the thought of catching it that he did not pay attention to his surroundings. In the early morning darkness, the hunter took careful steps towards his prey. One step. Another step. And another and suddenly he felt something around his right leg. He did not look at it. He thought it was a twig. He attempted to pull his leg away but whatever was around his leg wouldn't go away. The more he pulled his leg away the tighter the snare felt. The hunter struggled in silence.

The bearded monkey and the bald gorilla looked at each other with amazement and disbelief. The gorilla gave the monkey a thumps up. "We've got him. The trap has caught him."

"Ssshhh. Quiet."

The gorilla was impatient. His bulgy eyes shone in the morning darkness. There was a huge smile across his face. He whispered to the monkey. "Let's catch him before he escapes." The two raced down the tree and jumped onto the hunter.

"AAAARGHHH," he screamed behind his mask.

The hunter was shaking with fear when the gorilla pressed him hard on the ground.

"We've got you," the gorilla said with excitement. He removed the mask and looked straight into the eyes of the hunter. "So this is the man behind the mask."

"The man with only one face; the human face," the monkey mocked him.

"And where is your hat of life?" the gorilla asked. "And this is your idea of mutual respect and peaceful co-existence."

The hunter looked shocked and bewildered. He was breathing heavily.

The gorilla gave the monkey the bow, the arrows, the catapult and the mask. "Hide them somewhere in the forest."

The monkey collected the items and dashed into the darkness.

"Please let me go," the hunter pleaded.

"Look at the face of a liar, a murderer," the gorilla taunted him.

"If you release me I'll leave immediately. I promise."

"All the weapons are in a safe place," the monkey announced later.

"Now that you've been caught red-handed, what have you got to say?"

The hunter kept mum.

"If you want to be released, you have to talk."

The monkey stepped closer. "We believe in justice and fairness in *shakara* – but you have to talk. Are you guilty of deception and murder of animals?"

"Yes I am," the hunter admitted.

"Are you going to leave the forest immediately upon release?"

"Yes I will. I promise."

The two leaders withdrew and spoke in low voices. Moments later, the monkey said. "We'll let you go because you admitted you are guilty and you promised to leave the forest. If you are caught again the punishment will be severe. Do you understand?"

The gorilla quickly added. "We'll not be lenient next time."

"The punishment will be severe," the monkey repeated.

The hunter nodded.

The gorilla grudgingly removed the snare and released the hunter.

"Can I have my weapons back?" he demanded. "I'll only leave *shakara* with my weapons."

"We are not giving you the weapons. Just go," the gorilla shouted.

"The forest is incomplete without me. My future lies here."

The two leaders looked at each other.

"This human is stubborn," the monkey said laughing.

"You wouldn't know how to use the weapons anyway," the hunter bragged and limped away.

# CHAPTER SEVEN

# THE HUNTER RETREATS

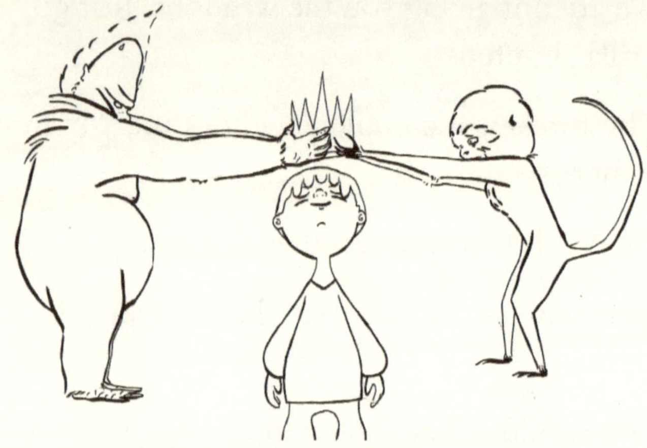

The hunter, followed by his loyal dog returned
to the cave. In his short sleep, the hunter had
a disturbing dream of being chased around by
some faceless beasts. These beasts eventually
caught him and he could not withstand the
strong body odour they released. He woke up
panting and covered his nose because he thought
he could still sense the strong smell.

The hunter wondered where things went wrong
for him. He could not admit that the animals
were intelligent enough to re-use the trap he
had once laid to catch him. "How could these
ignorant and stupid animals catch me?" He
concluded that what happened was a minor
setback. "I'll bounce back and dominate these

animals. Life will be great again. My dream will come true soon. The most beautiful days are ahead. *Shakara* will be mine forever. Somehow I will find a way and outmanoeuvre these ignorant animals."

When later he closed his eyes, he thought he heard through the secret tunnel the chants of the animals praising him: *Long live the king. Long live the conqueror! You shall rule over us forever!* He thought he saw the two leaders walk into the cave with a crown in their hands. "We are here to invite you to wear the crown as the esteemed leader of *shakara*. We're here to plead with you to be our leader. You have conquered *shakara* forest. We promise to be loyal and obedient to you the king of *shakara*. *Long live the king.*"

Meanwhile, in the forest, the monkey and gorilla settled down to examine the weapons. Rubbing his hands with excitement, the monkey whispered. "Let's copy the weapons before we give them back to him."

"How?" the gorilla asked scratching his bald head.

"Easy. First, let's understand how they work."

The two leaders first learnt how to use the bow and arrow. When they understood how it worked, they made their own bows and arrows. Then they turned their attention to the catapult.

"This is very hard to copy," the monkey conceded. Let's make it useless by destroying it."

"Why."

"So that when he wants to use it it'll not work."

"Yo monkey! Good thinking."

The monkey used a sharp object to cut the rubber of the catapult a bit. "This should do," he said.

"Let's make some beads to show him that we have symbols of power," the monkey suggested later."

"Yes, that we are the true leaders of the forest."

The two leaders made and decorated themselves with beads.

They then set out to give the hunter his weapons.

*"Long live animal thinking!*
*"Long live animal resilience!*
*"Long live animal ingenuity!*
*"Long live animal innovation!*
*"We shall never surrender to humans!*
*"We shall never be conquered by humans!*

The gorilla sang as they walked toward the cave.

*****

The monkey was the first to speak. "Here are your weapons."

"I knew you wouldn't know how to use them," said the hunter.

"You're right," replied the monkey smiling. "They are too difficult for us. We have no idea how to use them."

"Would you now leave the forest?" the gorilla suggested.

"I'm going nowhere," the hunter stubbornly stood his ground.

"But you promised to leave," insisted the monkey.

"I've every right to live here," he said brandishing the catapult.

"Yo monkey, let me sort this human out," the gorilla said with a clenched fist.

"Calm down," the monkey cautioned.

The hunter looked closely at the two animals. "What are you wearing?" he asked laughing.

"These are our symbols of power," the monkey answered.

"We are the real leaders of the forest," the gorilla added.

"I'm the king. I've conquered the forest," the hunter boasted, showing his catapult.

"We'll show you that we're the true leaders very soon," the monkey said.

"Shut up! Rubbish talk. You think a few beads around your head and a few beads around the gorilla's neck will make me leave the forest? These are not symbols of power." He showed them his catapult again. "This is power."

The gorilla charged forward angrily. The monkey pulled him back. "He's powerful and we are weak. He has weapons and we don't. But he has forgotten that no condition is permanent. It's just a matter of time before the hunter will become the hunted."

"Rubbish monkey talk."

# CHAPTER EIGHT

# THE HUNTER BECOMES THE HUNTED

Rubbing his hands in excitement, the monkey said the next day. "I think we're ready. We have given him enough chances to leave the forest. It's time for the hunter to be the hunted. It's time to chase him out of the forest."

The gorilla looked closely at the mask and laughed. "The human doesn't know what awaits him today."

When they were ready, the monkey and the gorilla hid behind bushes near the path they knew the hunter would take for his usual walk. As the hunter approached, the gorilla wore the mask, jumped out of the bushes and screamed. The hunter was scared. He started to run. The gorilla chased him, screaming loudly behind the mask. When the gorilla caught up with the hunter, he removed the mask laughing. The monkey who was armed with a bow and arrows had taken position on a branch above them.

"Why are you chasing me?" the hunter asked panting.

"For the very last time, leave this forest."

"I have the right to be here. The forest is incomplete without me."

"Your time is up," the gorilla said. "The forest will be a better place without you."

The gorilla signalled and ordered. "Yo monkey, give him one."

"No more talk of hunter becoming the hunted. Now it's time for action," the monkey took aim

and released an arrow. It went straight through the cone-shaped hat of the hunter.

The hunter was startled. He cowered in fear. "Oh my God," he exclaimed.

"That was a practice shot by the way," the gorilla said letting out a belly laugh.

The hunter stared in bewilderment. "Who taught you how to copy and use my weapons?" The monkey did not answer. He released another arrow that flew into the hat.

"The monkey can hit you wherever he wants," taunted the gorilla.

"Are you going to leave or not?" the monkey yelled.

The hunter remained adamant. "I'm going nowhere." He brought out his catapult.

"Hahaha! Hohoho! Hihihi!" the gorilla exclaimed loudly. "Go on. Use it."

The hunter hurriedly inserted a stone and aimed at the monkey. He pulled the catapult very hard and it snapped. The hunter looked shocked and confused.

"Your symbol of power is broken. You've lost. Just go," the monkey said and released an arrow that flew into his hat.

The hunter was scared. He cowered again. The two leaders of the forest laughed.

"We don't want to hurt you."

"We just want you to go away."

But will he?

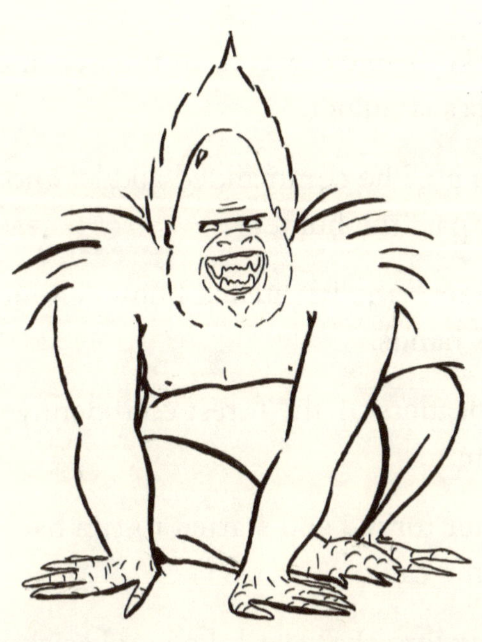

# AND FINALLY ...

The monkey came down from the tree and sat on the gorilla's shoulder.

"Off you go," he commanded and let another arrow fly past the hunter.

"I surrender," the frightened hunter shouted and raised his hands.

The two leaders of the forest confidently walked towards him.

The hunter turned and started to run back towards the cave.

"No going into the cave," the monkey shouted. "Out of the forest."

The monkey
jumped down
from the
shoulders of
the gorilla
and they
both chased
him.

From time to time, the monkey would let fly an
arrow near him.

"Hurray, the human is running away," yelled the
gorilla triumphantly.

The two leaders of the forest chased the hunter
from the forest!

That's how the hunter became the hunted!

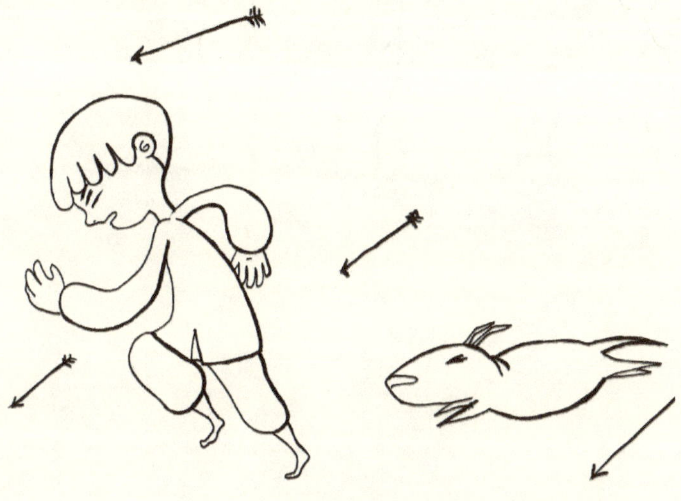

# THE END

## Also By Mohammed Umar

Samad in the Desert (2016)
978-0-9572084-3-8

Samad in the Forest (2015)
978-0-9572084-2-1

The Adventures of Jamil (2012)
978-0-9572084-0-7

Amina – A Novel (2005)
978-1-5922140-4-4

## Forthcoming

The Illegal Immigrant (2017)
978-0-9572084-5-2

Samad in the Savannah (2017)
978-0-9572084-6-9

For more information please visit our website
www.salaampublishing.com